This Faber book belongs to

· · · · · · · · · · · · · · · · · · · ·

For Max

First published in 2017 by Faber and Faber Limited
Bloomsbury House, 74–77 Great Russell Street, London WC1B 3DA

Designed by Faber and Faber
Printed in Malta
Text © Katie Blackburn, 2017
Illustrations © Richard Smythe, 2017
The rights of Katie Blackburn and Richard Smythe to be identified as author and illustrator of this work
respectively have been asserted in accordance with Section 77 of the Copyright, Designs and Patents Act 1988

A CIP record for this book is available from the British Library

ISBN 978–0–571–33443–8

10 9 8 7 6 5 4 3 2 1

→ A FABER PICTURE BOOK ←

Dozy Bear
and the
SECRET
of Food

Katie Blackburn

Illustrated by
Richard Smythe

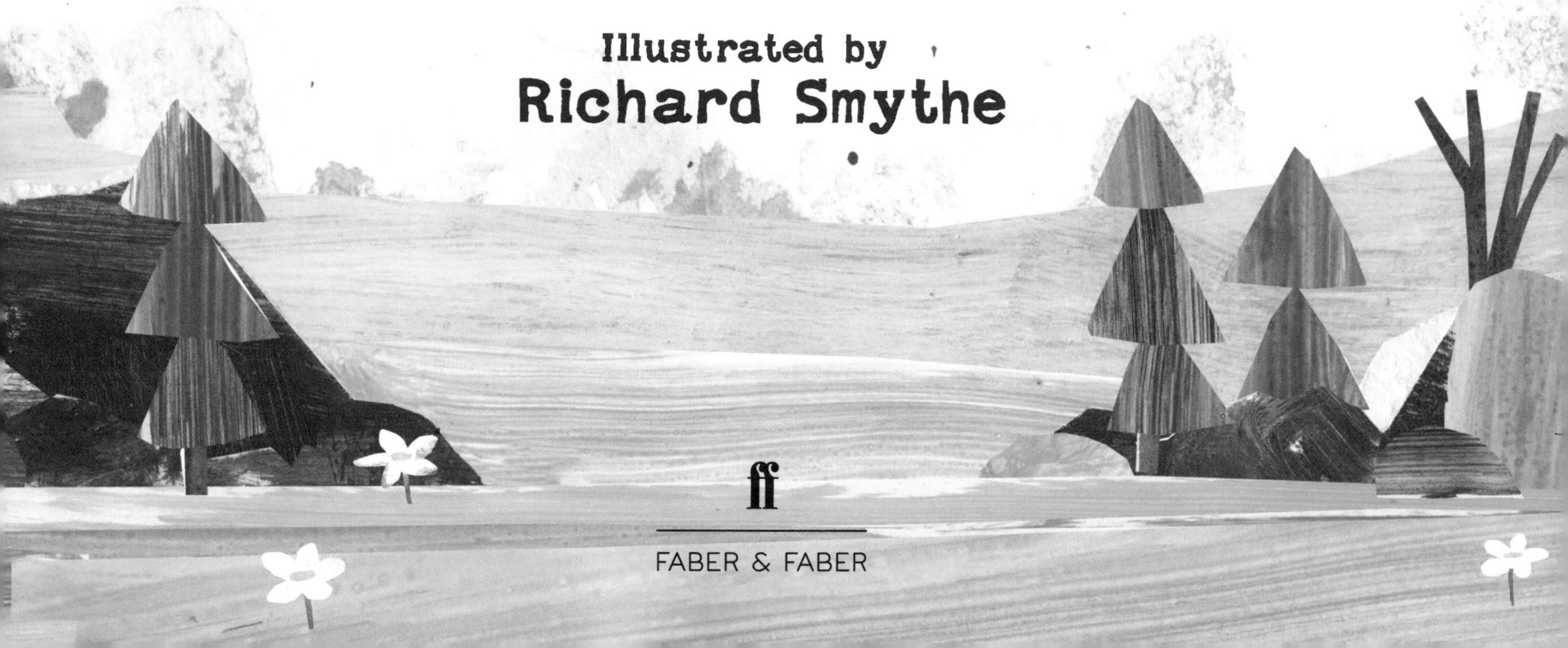

ff

FABER & FABER

The bears were finishing their lunch down by the river.

Chomp

Chomp

Chomp

Papa Bear licked his chops and rubbed his tummy with delight.

But little Dozy Bear wasn't happy . . .

'Mama, I *only* want fish,' he said, shaking his head
and waggling his paws, and pushing the food away.

'Oh, Dozy, do *try* something else,' said Mama Bear.

But Dozy would **NOT** . . .

And now all the other bears were fast asleep,
snoring loudly, and Dozy's tummy was **GRUMBLING.**

Dozy Bear was HUNGRY!

This is no good, he thought.
I'll find my **OWN** treats —
and off he trotted into the woods.

And that's how his adventure began!

It was cool under the trees.
Snuffle, snuffle.
Hedgehog was rolling something
across the ground.

'Look, Dozy,' she said.
'I've found an apple. Come and taste it!'
Dozy wasn't sure about apples . . . but he WAS hungry.

He sniffed it . . .
He licked it . . . He took
a very small bite.
'**Bah!**' He cried.

And another . . .
'**Boo!**'

And another . . .
'**Ah!**'

And another . . .
'**Oo!**'

It wasn't fish, but – '***Mm!***
TASTY!'

Snoozing in a tree, Owl opened
one eye. Then the other.
'Woo hoo!' Owl called.
'Are you hungry?
Have some blueberries!'

Dozy was up that tree, quick
as a flash, his nose twitching.
He stretched out a paw, he *loved*
blueberries. Didn't he? . . . **OH**.

'They're very *round*, Owl,' Dozy said.

'Yes, Dozy, but it doesn't matter what
they look like,' said Owl.
'They're **SCRUMPTIOUS!**'

Dozy sniffed a blueberry. He licked it. He
popped it in his mouth, and as he munched
he began to sing a funny little song . . .

'One bite – **Bah!**

Two bites – **Boo!**

Three bites – **Ah!**

Four bites – **Oo!**

Five bites – **Mm!**

Six bites – **Yum!**

Tastes
DELICIOUS,

fills my TUM!'

Dozy shook some blueberries on to the ground.

'Come on, Hedgehog, the more you eat,
the better they taste. Be brave like a lion!
Try some!' said Dozy.

'They're **SCRUMPTIOUS!**'

Hedgehog sniffed the blueberries. Then she licked them. Then she
popped one into her mouth and started singing Dozy's song.

'One bite – **Bah!**'
(She pulled a funny face.)

'Two bites – **Boo!**'
(Another funny face . . .)

'Three bites – **Ah!**

Four bites – **Oo!**

Five bites – **Mm!**

Six bites – **Yum!**

Tastes
DELICIOUS,

fills my TUM!'

'Bah, boo, ah, oo, hey you two!
Come and have a carrot,' called Rabbit,
as he finished off his lunch in the shade.

'I'm not sure, Rabbit,' Dozy said. 'They're so long —'
'— and *orange!*' added Hedgehog.

'Oh, you silly billies,' squeaked
Rabbit. 'Carrots are

SENSATIONAL!'

'You MUST try them.
Just give them a good
crunch, like a crocodile!'

So that's what they did . . .

'One bite – **Bah!**

Two bites – **Boo!**

Three bites – **Ah!**

Four bites – **Oo!**

Five bites – **Mm!**

Six bites – **Yum!**

Tastes **DELICIOUS, fills my TUM!'**

Crunch like
a crocodile!

Moose looked on from the water's edge,
slurping quietly.

'Dozy, Hedgehog, try these fresh green shoots,'
said Moose.

'Roll them round and round your mouth
like a hippo in a swamp!'

I wonder, thought Dozy. He dipped a paw into the cool water, and pulled out a bunch of shoots.

'Remember,' said Moose. 'Round and round your mouth, like a hippo!'

'One bite – **Bah!**

Two bites – **Boo!**

Three bites – **Ah!**

Four bites – **Oo** –
Join in, Hedgehog!' Dozy called.

'Five bites – **Mm!**

Six bites – **YUM!**

Tastes **DELICIOUS** —'

'Fills my tummy, tum, tum!'
sang Hedgehog.

And now Dozy realised the most **AMAZING** thing of all.

After six little tastes, it was ALL delicious.
Dozy had discovered **the Secret of Food!**

Food tastes good **IN DIFFERENT WAYS!**

It's **HOW** you eat it that matters, not what it looks like.
And the more you eat, the better it tastes!

Sniff it! Lick it! Take LOTS OF LITTLE BITES —
Like Dozy!

Be BRAVE like a lion!

PULL A FUNNY FACE like Hedgehog!

CRUNCH it like a crocodile!

ROLL it like a hippo!

How do YOU eat YOUR food?

Dozy sat in the shallows, feeling full and happy — when
SPLOSH! – a fish jumped out of the water
and into his lap.

A fish! His favourite food of all. But do you know, Dozy let that little fish bounce back into the water. He wasn't hungry any more!

Clever little bear.